Anonymous

A Catalogue of Rare & Curious Books, Illustrative of the English Drama and Early English Literature

Anatiposi

Anonymous

A Catalogue of Rare & Curious Books, Illustrative of the English Drama and Early English Literature

Reprint of the original.

1st Edition 2023 | ISBN: 978-3-38230-772-1

Anatiposi Verlag is an imprint of Outlook Verlagsgesellschaft mbH.

Verlag (Publisher): Outlook Verlag GmbH, Zeilweg 44, 60439 Frankfurt, Deutschland
Vertretungsberechtigt (Authorized to represent): E. Roepke, Zeilweg 44, 60439 Frankfurt, Deutschland
Druck (Print): Books on Demand GmbH, In de Tarpen 42, 22848 Norderstedt, Deutschland

S. LEIGH SOTHEBY & JOHN WILKINSON,

WELLINGTON STREET, STRAND.

CATALOGUE

OF

RARE & CURIOUS BOOKS,

ILLUSTRATIVE OF

THE ENGLISH DRAMA

AND

EARLY ENGLISH LITERATURE.

A CATALOGUE

OF

RARE & CURIOUS BOOKS,

ILLUSTRATIVE OF

THE ENGLISH DRAMA

AND

EARLY ENGLISH LITERATURE;

INCLUDING

SOME CHOICE EDITIONS OF THE WORKS

OF

SHAKESPEARE, ROBERT GREENE, BARNABY RICH,

AND OTHERS,

EARLY ENGLISH POETRY, NOVELS,

AND

OTHER RARE BOOKS.

~~~~~~~~~~~~~~~

WHICH WILL BE SOLD BY AUCTION,

BY MESSRS.

S. LEIGH SOTHEBY & JOHN WILKINSON,

AUCTIONEERS OF LITERARY PROPERTY AND WORKS ILLUSTRATIVE OF THE FINE ARTS,

AT THEIR HOUSE, 3, WELLINGTON ST., STRAND,

On Monday, 13th June, 1859,

AT ONE O'CLOCK PRECISELY.

————————

MAY BE VIEWED TWO DAYS PREVIOUS, AND CATALOGUES HAD.

PRINTED BY J. E. ADLARD, BARTHOLOMEW CLOSE.

CONDITIONS OF SALE.

I. The highest Bidder to be the Buyer; and if any dispute arise between Bidders, the Lot so disputed shall be immediately put up again, provided the seller cannot decide the said dispute.

II. No Person to advance less than 6d.; above Ten Shillings, 1s.; above Five Pounds, 2s. 6d.; and so on.

III. The Purchasers to give in their Names and Places of Abode, and to pay down 10s. in the Pound, if required, in Part of Payment of the Purchase-money; in default of which, the Lot or Lots purchased to be immediately put up again and re-sold.

IV. The Lots to be taken away, at the Buyer's Expense, immediately after the conclusion of the Sale; in default of which, Messrs. S. LEIGH SOTHEBY and JOHN WILKINSON will not hold themselves responsible if lost, stolen, damaged, or otherwise destroyed, but they will be left at the sole risk of the Purchaser. If, at the expiration of ONE WEEK after the conclusion of the Sale, the Books or other property are not cleared or paid for, they will then be catalogued for immediate sale, and the expense, the same as if re-sold, will be added to the amount at which the books were bought. Messrs. S. LEIGH SOTHEBY and JOHN WILKINSON will have the option of re-selling the Lots uncleared either by public or private sale, without any notice being given to the defaulter.

V. The Books are presumed to be perfect, unless otherwise expressed; but if, upon collating, any should prove defective, the Purchaser will be at liberty to take or reject them, provided they are returned within ONE WEEK after the conclusion of the Sale, when the Purchase-money will be *returned*.

VI. The sale of any Book or Books is not to be set aside on account of any stained or short leaves of text or plates, want of list of plates, or on account of the publication of any subsequent Volume, Supplement, Appendix, or Plates. All the Manuscripts, Autographs, all Magazines and Reviews, all Books in Lots, and all Tracts in Lots or Volumes, will be sold with all faults, imperfections, and errors of description. The sale of any lot of Prints or Drawings not to be set aside on account of any error in the enumeration of the numbers stated, or Errors of Description.

VII. No IMPERFECT BOOKS will be taken back, unless a note accompanies each Book, stating its imperfections, with the Number of Lot and date of the Sale at which the same was purchased.

VIII. To prevent inaccuracy in delivery, and inconvenience in the settlement of the purchases, no Lot can on any account be removed during the time of Sale.

IX. Upon failure of complying with the above Conditions, the Money required and deposited in part of Payment shall be forfeited; and *if any loss is sustained in the re-selling of such books as are not cleared or paid for, all charges on such Re-sale shall be made good by the Defaulters at this Sale.*

Gentlemen who cannot attend the Sale may have their Commissions faithfully executed by their humble Servants,

S. LEIGH SOTHEBY & JOHN WILKINSON,

Wellington Street, Strand.

A CATALOGUE

OF

𝔠𝔲𝔯𝔦𝔬𝔲𝔰 𝔈𝔞𝔯𝔩𝔶 𝔈𝔫𝔤𝔩𝔦𝔰𝔥 𝔏𝔦𝔱𝔢𝔯𝔞𝔱𝔲𝔯𝔢, &𝔠.

LOT

1 Old Plays, in quarto   *a parcel*

2 Hale (W. H.) Domesday of St. Paul's of the year 1222, or, Registrum de Visitatione Maneriorum per Robertum Decamem   *4to. Cam. Soc.* 1858

3 Jordan (Thomas) Nursery of Novelties in Variety of Poetry, planted for the delightful Leisures of Nobility and Ingenuity, *of extreme rarity, but imperfect*   *8vo.*

4 Rogers (Francis) Sermon of Love, preached at Folkestone, a Maior Towne in Kent, *8vo.* 1613—Muses Farewell to Popery and Slavery, Poems, Satyrs, &c. *8vo.* 1689— A Sermon upon Hospitality, preached at Tunbridge in Kent, *8vo.* 1708

5 Annotations illustrative of the Plays of Shakespeare, 2 *vol. 8vo.* 1819—The Chester Plays, *vol.* 2—Wright (T.) Anglo-Saxon and other Vocabularies, *text only,* 1858

6 Andromana or the Merchant's Wife, the Scæne Iberia, by J. S.   4to. *Lond.* 1660

   ** "This copy (last leaf MS.) sold at Rhodes' sale for £1 15*s.* The only other copy cited by Lowndes (under *Shirley*) sold for £3 1*s.* It is very scarce."—*MS. note.*

7 The Overthrow of Stage-Plays, by the Way of Controversie betwixt D. Gager and D. Rainoldes, wherein all the reasons that can be made for them are notably refuted, *very rare, but title and two or three leaves slightly defective,* 1600—The State of the Imperiall Court of the Emperour Ferdinand, 1637—Salamandrologia, 1683, *plates* —Heywood (Thomas) Fair Maid of the West, or a Girle worth Gold, *both parts, but wants title to second part,* 1631—Jocasta, a Tragedie from Euripides by George Gascoigne and Francis Kinwelmershe of Grayes Inne, 1566, 𝔟𝔩𝔞𝔠𝔨-𝔩𝔢𝔱𝔱𝔢𝔯, *from Gascoigne's Works*

8 Weldon (A.) Court and Character of King James, 8vo. 1689—
A Treatise of Humane Reason   12mo. 1675. 2 vol.

9 History of Little Goody Two-Shoes, otherwise called Mrs.
Margery Two Shoes, with the means by which she ac-
quired her Learning and Wisdom, *front*.   18mo.   1768

10 Short Account of the Proceedings of the College of Physicians,
1697—Vindication of Dryden, 1673—Reflections on the
Duke of Guise, 1683—Occasional Paper, No. 9, on the
Danger of Going to Plays, 1698—De Ratione Motus
Musculorum, 1664—Causes of the Discontents, 1721

11 Hawes (W.) Account of the Late Dr. Goldsmith's Illness, 1774
—De Medicorum, &c. 1726— Pompey, a Tragedy, *uncut*,
1663—Love for Love, 1695

12 Beaumont and Fletcher's King and no King, 1631, *uncut*—
Destruction of Jerusalem, 1703—Massinger's New Way to
Pay Old Debts, FIRST EDITION, 1633—The Recruiting
Officer, *n. d.*

13 Old Plays, in quarto   *a parcel*

14 Seasonable Warning to all Hardened Sinners, preached at
Newington next Hyth, in the County of Kent, 1702—
Satyrs of Boileau imitated, 1696—Impartial History of
Plots, 1696—The Emperour and the Empire, 1682—
Observations on the United Provinces, 1680—Life and
Death of Sir M. Hale, 1682

15 Heywood (Thomas) Foure Prentises of London, with the Con-
quest of Jerusalem, as it hath beene divers times acted at
the Red Bull by the Queenes Majesties with good applause, *large wood-cut*
very rare, but two or three leaves are slightly defective
4to.   1632

16 Observations on Sorbier's Voyage into England, 1665—Ward's
Wit and Wisdom, 1673—Journey to Naples, with the
Frauds of Romish Monks and Priests, 1691—Man with-
out Passion, 1675—Perswasive to Conformity, 1670—
The Nomenclator or Remembrancer of A. Junius, 1585

17 Observations on Homer and Virgil, 1672—Reflections on Good
Luck and Ill Luck, 1699—Mathematical Magic, 1691—
Odes of Horace, in English verse, 1638—Memoirs of
Christendom, 1692

18 Titus and Gissippus, the Banquet of the Gods, old English
Poetical Tales, *believed to be perfect, but sold with all
faults*—The Tragedy of Hamlet, *reprint of ed.* 1603

19 Pourtract of Old Age, 1676—Cleaveland's Poems, *port.* 1677—
Elements of Speech, 1669—The City and Country Purchaser, 1680—Walker (W.) Treatise of English Particles,
1663

20 Honesty in Distress, in Verse, 1710—Visits from the Shades, 1704—Worledge (E.) Resurrection, a Poem, 1716—Count Piper's Packet, being a choice and curious Collection of Manuscript Papers in Prose and Verse that were found bundled under a bench upon Duke Humphrey's Walk in St. James's Park, 1732—Pope (A.) Temple of Fame, 1715—Pope (A.) Essay on Criticism, 1713—Preston (—) Æsop at the Bear Garden, 1715 ; and others   *in* 1 *vol.*

21 Hughes (W.) Flower Garden, showing how Flowers are to be ordered, 1672—The European Mercury, describing High Wages and Stages, 1641—Aristippus, a Discourse concerning the Court, 1659—Compleat Statesman, *port*. 1683 —The Life of Admiral de Ruyter, *port*.   1677

22 The Dreadful Character of a Drunkard, or the Odious and beastly Sin of Drunkenness described and condemned, black-letter, *woodcut, Printed for W. Thackeray,* 1681— A Warning-Piece to the Slothful, Idle, Careless, Drunken, &c., black-letter, with A Perswasion to Temperance, *in verse, Printed for William Thackeray, in Duck-lane,* 1678
12*mo.   in* 1 *vol.*

    ⁎ Very rare and curious.   Perfect, but some of the margins slightly cut.

23 Art-Union Prize Annual   *folio.*   1845

24 MOLYNEUX. An Account of the Family and Descendants of Sir Thomas Molyneux, Knt., Chancellor of the Exchequer in Ireland to Queen Elizabeth
privately printed, very scarce, a privately printed pedigree of the Molyneux family inserted   4to.   Evesham, 1820

25 Life and Death of Alexander, 1674—The History of Isuf Bassa, 1684—Help to English History, 1641—The Voyage of Italy, 1670—Medulla Historiæ, 1679—Comparison of Eloquence, 1672—An English Expositor, 1684—Principles of Law, 1661—The Guardian's Instruction, 1688—The Life of Donna Olimpia, 1667—Letters from Switzerland, 1686 —Langbaine's Dramatic Poets, *imperfect, but with early MS. notes,* 1691

26 Richardson (C.) New Dictionary of the English Language, 4 *vol. a few leaves defective*   4*to.*   1835

27 Elliptical or Azimuthal Horologiography, 4*to.* 1654—Willis (T.) Affections, *portrait,* 1670—Divine History of Genesis, 1670—Practical Divinity of the Papists, 1678

28 Romulus and Tarquin, 1638—Downing's Discourse, 1672— The Commonwealth's Man Unmasked, 1694—A Relation of the Siege of Candia, 1670—The Plot in a Dream, 1681 A Full Account of the Siege of Stretin, 1678—Grotius's Annals, 1665

1 6 0 29 Decker (Thomas) Dove and the Serpent, in which is contained
a large description of all such points and principles as
tend either to conversation, &c. *prose intermixed with
verse* 4to. *T. C. for Laurence L' Isle*, 1614

⁎⁎ This curious tract, of which we can trace no other copy,
is signed by D. T., possibly Decker, who sometimes re-
versed his initials, but we have only conjecture to attribute
it to that prolific writer, who wrote in a serious as well as
in a comic style.

3 6 30 May (John) Declaration of the Estate of Clothing now used
within this Realme of England 4to. 1613

3 31 Shirley (James) Triumph of Beautie, as it was personated by
some young Gentlemen for whom it was intended at a
private Recreation 12mo. 1646

⁎⁎ The Roxburghe copy £1 3s., and the Reed copy £1 6s.,
are the only ones mentioned by Lowndes.

1 11 0 32 JEW. The Wandering Jew telling Fortunes to Englishmen,
large woodcut, imprint cut off *circa* 1640

⁎⁎ An excessively curious book of characters. The present
was Reed's copy, bought at his sale by Heber for £2 2s.
Only three copies are known.

12 33 Breton (Nicolas) Wits Private Wealth stored with choise commodities to content the minde, *title in facsimile*
4to. *Tho. Creede for John Tapp*, 1615

4 34 Mackenzie's Moral Gallantry, 1669—Boyle's New Experiments,
1681—Memoirs of the Duke de la Rochefoucault, 1683—
The Drudge, a Piece of Gallantry, *interspersed with verse,*
1673—Apiarium, or a Discourse of Bees, 1678, *from
Worlidge's Husbandry*

2 35 Sanderson (R.) Lectures on Oaths, 1655—Manchester al Mondo,
1635—Reflections on Eloquence, 1672—Mercury, or the
Secret and Swift Messenger, 1694—Anacreon done into
English, 1683—Massinger's Roman Actor, 1722, and
other plays 8vo.

16 36 Nares (R.) Glossary, *new edition* 2 vol. *Russell Smith*, 1859

7 6 37 S. (W.) Instructions for the Increasing of Mulberie Trees, and
the breeding of silke-wormes for the making of Silke in
this Kingdome, *woodcuts*
scarce 4to. *By E. A. for Eleazar Edgar*, 1609

6 6 38 Gauden (Bp.) A Discourse of Auxiliary Beauty, or Artificiall
Handsomenesse
FIRST EDITION, *original binding* 1656

⁎⁎ Ant. a Wood ascribes this work to Dr. Gauden. It is
often attributed to Bp. Jeremy Taylor, and occasionally to
Obadiah Walker, whose share in the volume was probably
limited to the "Satyrical Censures," as given in the
edition of 1662.

39 Grew (N.) Anatomy of Vegetables, 1672—Baker's Poems, Hicathrift, Duellum inter Juvenem quendam fortissimum, cui nomen Hicathrift, et gigantem ferocissimum qui publicos Agros (vulgo Marshland Smee) occupaverat, 1697—Grandeur of France, 1673—Compendious View of Tumults, 1685

40 Heywood (J.) Three Hundreth of Epigrammes uppon three hundreth Proverbes, and a fifth and sixte hundred of Epigrammes ; black letter, *imperfect*, 1576—Rights of the Kingdom or Customs, &c. 4to. 1682

41 Rusden (Moses, *Bee-master to Charles II*) Further Discovery of Bees, *plates*   *Printed for the Author*, 1679

42 Somner (William) Treatise of the Roman Ports and Forts in Kent, *portrait*   Oxford, 1693

43 Whitelocke (Sir J.) Liber Famelicus   Camd. Soc. 1858

44 Holles (Lord) Grand Question and the Case of Thomas Skinner, complaining of the East India Company, *with MS. notes, and made up with MS.* 1669—Vulgar Errors by Battell, 1683—Tarlton's Remedy for the Warres, 1648—Discourse of Parliaments, 1677—Langford on Fruit Trees, 1681

45 Cooper (W. D.) Savile Correspondence, Letters from Henry Savile, temp.Charles II, and from his brother, the Marquess of Halifax   4to. Camd. Soc. 1858

46 Cassandra, the Fam'd Romance, 1652—The Mysterie of Rhetorique, 1657—Account of the Siege of Stretin, 1678—The Prince of Conde, 1675—Milton's Defence of the People of England, 1692—Bartholinus de Unicornu, 1678

47 Hopperi (J.) in Veram Jurisprudentiam libri octo, *with more than one autograph signature, two pages of MS. and numerous marginal notes, in the handwriting of the celebrated Gabriel Harvey*   8vo. Colon. 1580
  ⁎ The autograph on the title is,—-Gabrielis Harvey, 1580.

48 Bell (R.) Poets—Wyatt, Greene and Marlowe, Surrey   3 vol.

49 Grimaldi Shakespeare, 1853, and other Shakespeariana—Piso's Conspiracy, a Tragedy, 1676

50 Decker (Thomas) Wonder of a Kingdome   4to. 1636

51 Lamothe (C. G.) Inspiration of the New Testament, 1694—Boyle's Experiments, 1664—Speculum Juventutis or a Mirror of Youth, 1671—Mun's Englands Benefit by Foreign Trade, 1698—Two Letters of Advice, 1691

52 Playford (J.) Catch that Catch Can, or the Musical Companion, Glees, Ayres, &c.
  rare, but imperfect   4to. 1667

53 Way to True Happinesse leading to the Gate of Knowledge, 1642—Sternhold and Hopkins' Whole Book of Psalmes collected into English Meeter, 1661.   8vo. *in 1 vol.*

_.3 /. 6 54 Monk's Hood Pull'd Off, or the Capuchin Friar Described, *front.* 1671—Boyle on Human Blood, 1684—An Exact Abridgement of the Trials, 1690—Jenner's Prerogative of Primogeniture, 1685—Boyle's Origine of Formes and Qualities, 1677

—/. 6 55 **Transactions** of the Royal Society of Literature, *vol VI, part* 1 —Précis Analytique des Travaux de l'Académie Impériale de Rouen, 1857   2 *vol.*

_2 /. 6 56 Ovid's Metamorphosis by G. Sandys, 1678—The Key of Historie, 1635—Treatise of the Interest of Princes, 1641—Chamberlayne's Present State of England, 1679—Taylor's Measures of Friendship, *portrait,* 1684

_.3 - 57 Reflections on Varilla's History, 1686—Dialogue Between a Popish Priest and an English Protestant, 1670—The Italian Couvert, newes from Italy, 1639—Heylin's Help to English History, 1671—Colbert's Ghost, 1684—Compleat Politician, 1656

_.5 - 58 Markham (Gervase) Souldiers Accidence, or an Introductorie into Military Discipline, with the Cavallarie or Trayning of Horses
     scarce   4*to.* 1625

—4 - 59 Marlowe (Christopher) Troublesome Raigne and Lamentable Death of Edward the Second, with the Tragicall Fall of Proud Mortimer; also, the Life and Death of Peirs Gavestone   4*to. Henry Bell,* 1622

—4 - 60 Turnebull (Charles) Perfect and Easie Treatise of the Use of the Cælestial Globe, for the unskilful in the studie of Astronomie, *uncut, slightly wormed*
     exceedingly rare   *Symon Waterson,* 1597

- 2 - 61 Burton (R.) Wars in England, Scotland, and Ireland, 1683— Adam out of Eden, 1659—Treatise on the bitter Purging Salt, 1697—The New State of England, 1694—The Princess of Cleves, 1679

_.3 - 62 Waterhous (E.) Apologie for Learning, 1653—Zayde, a Spanish Romance, *front.* 1678—Boyle's Experiments, 1674— Loyal Poems and Satyrs, 1685—The Four Ages of England, a Poem, 1675

- 3 - 63 Saul at Endor, 1692—Doctrine of the Bible, 1687—Rawleigh's Marrow of Historie, 1650—A Serious Proposal to the Ladies, 1695—Magna Charta, 1618—The Cid, a Tragi-Comedy, 1650

- .3 - 64 History of Catiline, 1684—Raleigh's Arts of Empire, 1692— Carter (M.) Honor Redivivus, or an Analysis of Honour and Armory, 1655—D. (J.) Polemicall Short Discussions, 1651

- 2 - 65 Pasquin Risen from the Dead, or his own Relation of a late Voyage he made to the other World in a Discourse with his friend Marforio   8*vo.* 1674

_2.6_ 66 Heylyn (P.) English History, 1680—Machiavel's Discourses, 1636—The Ephesian and Cimmerian Matrons, 1668—An English Expositor, 1686

— _5.6_ 67 Essay in Defence of the Female Sex, in which are inserted the Characters of a Pedant, a Beau, &c. *cur. front. of the Compleat Beau* 1697

— _.3_— 68 Scarronides, or Virgile Travestie, a Mock Poem, 1678—History of Justin, 1664—Ascham's Discourse on Government, 1648—The Mysterie of Rhetorique Unvail'd, 1657

_5-2.6_ 69 Middleton (T.) Trick to Catch the Old One, as it hath beene lately Acted by the Children of Paules
    a very fine copy   4to.
              At London, Printed by George Eld, and are to be sold at his house in Fleete Lane at the signe of the Printers Presse, 1608

    ** This is the only copy known with this imprint.

—_6.6_ 70 W. (I.) Charitable Physician and Apothecary   4to.   1639

—_2.6_ 71 Barrey (Lo.) Ram Alley or Merrie Trickes, a Comedy divers times heretofore acted by the Children of the King's Revels
                                  4to.   *G. Eld,* 1611

—_2.6_ 72 Travels through Flanders, Holland, &c., 1693—Poems by a late Scholar of Eaton, 1689—The Painters' Voyage of Italy, *front. but no portraits,* 1679—The Patriarch Unmonarch'd, *front.* 1681—Charter of Charles II to the City of London
                                        5 *vol.*

— _1.6_ 73 War between the English and Dutch, 1671—A Treatise of Humane Reason, 1675—Tudor Prince of Wales, a Novel, 1678—The Siege of Antwerp, *n. d.*   4 *vol.*

— _4_ — 74 The Abyssinian Philosophy, 1697—Account of John the Third, King of Poland, 1684—A Description of Candia, 1670—The Situation of Paradise, 1694   4 *vol.*

— _2_ — 75 Europe a Slave, 1681—The Faithful Analist, *n. d.*—The Modern Courtier, 1687—Directions for a Godly Life, 1680—The French Gardener, 1672   5 *vol.*

—_3.6_ 76 An Augustine Friar his Epistles, 1673—A Discourse of Constancy, *front.* 1654—Seasonable Reflections on Scoffing, 1676—Mathematical Magick, 1691   4 *vol.*

— _6_ — 77 Wright (T.) History of Ireland, 27 *parts*

—_3.6_ 78 Butler (S.) Works, ed. Bell   3 *vol.*   1855

— _1_ — 79 Butler's Ghost, or Hudibras the Fourth Part, with Reflections upon these times, *in verse*   1682

—_5_— 80 Shakespeare.—The Universal Passion, a Comedy altered from Much Ado about Nothing, *two copies, 8vo.* 1737—Henry the Fourth, from a contemporary MS. *Shak. Soc.* 1845—Account of the Incidents of the Tempest, 1809, from the Variorum

81 Shakespeare. Love Betray'd, or the Agreeable Disapointment, partly taken from Twelfth Night, 4to. 1703—The Jew of Venice, a Comedy, 4to. 1701—Measure for Measure, or Beauty the Best Advocate, altered from Shakespeare, 4to. 1700

82 Shakespeare. The Fairy Queen, an Opera represented at the Queen's Theatre, altered from the Midsummer Night's Dream   4to. 1692

83 Shakespeare. Seven preliminary leaves from the third folio edition   fol. 1664

84 Fage (John) Speculum Ægrotorum, the Sicke Mens Glasse, whereunto is annexed a treatise of the four Humors
   black letter, *with a curious Epilogue of the Author in verse*
           4to. *William Lugger upon Holborne-bridge*, 1606
   ₊ Another copy, in the Malone collection, is the only one we can trace

85 Shakespeare. The Ingratitude of a Common-Wealth, or the Fall of Caius Martius Coriolanus, *altered from Shakespeare two copies*   4to. 1682

86 Shakespeare (W.) Works, edited from ed. 1623, with various readings, notes, &c., by Richard Grant White, *vol. 2 to 5, all published*   8vo. *Boston, U. S.* 1857

87 Shakespeare. Hamlet, ed. 1603, *reprint, uncut*   8vo. 1825

88 Shakespeare (W.) Julius Cæsar as acted at the Theatre Royal
                                                        4to. 1691

89 Shakespeare. Another edition   4to. n. d. BARTON.

90 Shakespeare (W.) Macbeth, a Tragedy, with all the Alterations, Do. Amendments, and New Songs   4to. 1695

91 Troilus and Cressida, or Truth Found Out too Late, a Tragedy as it is acted at the Duke's Theatre, 4to. 1679—Shadwell (Thomas) History of Timon of Athens, the Man Hater, as it is acted at the Duke's Theatre, 4to. 1688

92 SHAKESPEARE'S JESTS, *no title*   8vo. *circa* 1770
   ₊ It is difficult to account for the extreme rarity of this quaint but very gross collection, in which a number of anecdotes are fathered on Shakespeare. Only two copies besides the present have occurred to our notice, and one of those also wants the title. It does not appear to be noticed in any list of Shakesperiana.

93 Shakespeare. Facsimile of the Title-page of the First Edition of BARTON Lear, 1608, *two copies*—Facsimile of the Anecdote respecting Shakespeare in Jocabella, or the Cabinet of Conceits, *six copies*

94 Canary Islands. A Proclamation prohibiting the Importation of wines of the Growth of the Canary Islands
   black letter   1666

95 Shakespeare. An Excellent Ballad, intituled the Constancy of Susanna, to an excellent new Tune, Licensed according to Order, *woodcut, the ballad quoted in Twelfth Night,* an early rude sheet copy, printed probably about 1670

96 Shakespeare. Sheet facsimile of the various autographs of the poet, published by the late T. Rodd, *two copies*   1843

97 Bert (Edmund) Approved Treatise of Hawkes and Hawking, divided into three Bookes, *woodcut, corner of title torn very scarce*   4to. 1619

98 Shakespeare. Facsimile of the last page of the first edition of Hamlet, 1603, *two copies, one on India paper* (only six copies lithographed by Mr. Ashbee)

99 Bell (R.) Songs from the Dramatists   8vo.   1854

100 Kirkman (F.) Wits, or Sport upon Sport, in selected Pieces of Drollery, *8vo. very imperfect,* 1673 ; also, a fragment of the same work

101 Shakespeare (W.) Whole Contention between the Two Famous Houses of York and Lancaster, *a fragment of twelve leaves*   4to. 1619

102 Jackson (Thomas) London's New Yeeres Gift, or the Uncouching of the Foxe, *see MS. notes by Dr. Bliss extremely rare*   4to. 1609

103 Saltonstall (Wye) Picturæ Loquentes, or Pictures drawne forth in Characters, *with a Poem of a Maid a remarkably fine copy*   12mo. 1635

** This edition contains thirty-eight characters ; the poem is printed with woodcuts, top and bottom, and occupies 15 pages

104 Kirkman (F) Wits, *a large fragment*   1673

105 Royal Charter of Confirmation granted by King James II to the Trinity House, Deptford, *front.*   1685

106 Thieves. The Fraternitye of Vacabondes, as wel of ruflyng Vacabondes as of beggerly, 1575, *uncut   reprint,* 1813

107 Peacham (H.) Valley of Varietie, *no front.*   1638

108 Treatise of Use and Custome, 4to. 1638—Charlton (Walter) Natural History of Nutrition, Life, and Voluntary Motion, 4to. 1659

109 Libri (G.) Catalogue of Manuscripts ; and others   3 *parcels*

110 Ludlow (Edmund) Memoirs, *portrait*   3 vol. 1698

111 Prideaux (N.) Introduction for Reading Histories   4to. Oxford, 1664

112 Act of Tonnage, 1675—Reflections on Eloquence, 1672—Religio Stoici, by Sir G. Mackenzie, *Edinburgh,* 1665—Satyrs on the Jesuits, *in verse,* 1681   4 vol.

113 Collection of the Debates in 1694 and 1695   4to.   1695

114 Fulbecke (W.) Abridgement, or rather a Bridge of Roman Histories to passe the neerest way from Titus Livius   4to. 1608

2

—/— 115 Polybius, translated by Sir H. Shears   2 *vol.*   1698

—//— 116 Jorden (E.) Discourse of Naturall Bathes, especially of our Bathes at Bathe in Sommersetshire, 1631—The Schoole of Salernes, black letter, *intermixed with verses*, 1617—Certaine Workes of Chirurgerie, newlye compiled and published by Thomas Gale, black letter, 1586—A Rich Storehouse or Treasury for the Diseased, black letter, 1596   4*to. in* 1 *vol.*

—//— 117 Sutcliffe (M.) Practice, Proceedings, and Lawes of Armes, described out of the doings of most valiant and expert Captaines

black letter   4*to.*   *C. Barker*, 1593

—/— 118 Culpeper (N.) London Dispensatory   8*vo.*   1659

** See an allusion to Banks' Horse at p. 210.

—2/ 119 Plat (Sir Hugh) Garden of Eden   12*mo.*   1653

—/— 120 James I. Speech in Parliament, with the Discovery of the Treason of the Gunpowder Plot   4*to.*   1605

—2/h 121 Meaux (B.) Maxims and Reflections on Plays   8*vo.*   1699

—2— 122 Howell (James) Lexicon Tetraglotton, the part containing the Lexicon, *front. valuable for archaisms*   *fol.*   1660

—4— 123 Douce (F.) Illustrations of Shakespeare   1839

—// 124 Mynshull (G.) Essayes and Characters of a Prison and Prisoners, written by G. M. of Grayes Inn, gent., with some new additions, *woodcut*

    4*to.*   *M. Walbancke*, 1638

—/0 125 Wadsworth (James) English Spanish Pilgrime, or a new Discoverie of Spanish Popery, and Jesuiticall Stratagems, *first edition*

very scarce   4*to.*   1629

** This first edition was unknown to Wood or Watt.

—/— 126 Sherwood (R.) Dictionarie English and French   *fol.*   1632

—2/h 127 Long (T.) History of Popish Plots, 1684—D. (E.) Machiavel's Discourses upon the first Decade of Livy, 1636—History of the Managements of Cardinal Mazarine, tom. I, part 2, and part 3, 1672-3   4 *vol.*

—2— 128 Norris (J.) Miscellanies, Poems, &c. 1692—Two Discourses on the Wits of Men, &c. 1669—The Sage Senator, 1660—Of Education of Young Gentlemen, 1673—Wingate's Abridgement, 1666

—2— 129 State Mysteries of the Jesuites, 1623—The Prerogative of the Parliaments in England, 1628—A Letter to Mr. T. H. late Minister now Fugitive, 1609

—/— 130 Catholics. An Answere to Certaine Scandalous Papers scattered abroad under Colour of a Catholicke Admonition

    4*to.*   *R. Barker*, 1606

_ 2 6_ 131 Kean (C.) Tempest, 1857—Henry the Eighth, 1855—Winter's *BARTON.*
Tale, 1856, *two copies*

_2-13-0_ 132 Shakespeare. The Legend of Shakespeare's Crab Tree, with a
descriptive Account showing its relation to the Poet's
traditional history, *illustrated with plates*
4to. *Privately printed*, 1857

_ (0._ 133 Pamphlets, some Shaksperian—Staunton's and Knight's
Shakespeare, various parts, &c. 3 *parcels*

_ /_ 134 Percivale (R.) Dictionarie in Spanish and English, enlarged by
Minsheu, with contemporary MS. notes
fol. E. Bollifant, 1599

_/-/_ 135 Shakespeare (W.) Troublesome Raigne of King John, containing the Entrance of Lewis the French King's sonne, with
the Poysoning of King John by a Monke
an unusually large copy, but incomplete in both parts
4to. *Aug. Mathewes for J. Dewe*, 1622.

_ /_ 136 Shakespeare (W.) First Part of the Contention of the Two
Famous Houses of Yorke and Lancaster, with the Death
of the good Duke Humfrey, *a large fragment* 1619

_-12-_ 137 Tobacco. James I's Counterblaste to Tobacco
an early quarto edition, without title.
⁎ This appears to be a contemporary separate quarto edition,
unnoticed by bibliographers.

138 Gayton (E.) Wil Bagnal's Ghost, or the Merry Devil of Gad-
munton in his Perambulation of the Prisons of London,
_4-6-0_ *in prose and verse, fine copy of a scarce and curious, but
exceedingly gross work* 4to. 1655
⁎ Bindley's copy sold for £3 6s.

139 Twici (William) Art of Hunting, by William Twici, huntsman
to King Edward the Second, printed from MS. Phillipps,
_/-15-0_ with preface, translation, notes, &c. *plates*
4to. *Daventry*, 1843
⁎ Only 25 copies privately printed. The present is believed
to be the only one that has occurred for public sale.

140 Annotations of Johnson and Steevens and the various Com- *BARTON.*
_-/-_ mentators upon Shakespeare's Richard the Second, *large
paper and uncut*, 1787—Reed's Shakespeare, vols. II and
III 8vo. 1803

141 Gayton (Edmund) Art of Longevity, or a Diælecticall Institution,
_- /0-_ *in verse, a fine copy, but slightly wormed, rare*
4to. *Printed for the Author*, 1659
⁎ Sold at Bindley's sale for £4 12s.

142 Buchanan (George) De Jure Regni apud Scotos Dialogus, 4to.
_- 2-6_ 1579—Venner (T.) Via Recta ad Vitam Longam, with a
Compendious Treatise of the famous Baths of Bathe, 1628

143 Divine Judgment and Mercy Exemplified in surprising instances
of John Duncalf of Kings Swinford, the Earl of Rochester,
_- 3-6_ *front. and woodcuts* 1746

144 Shaw (S.) Words made Visible, a play represented in a Country School, *both parts* 1679

145 Holliband (C.) Treatise for Declining of Verbes (*useful for archaisms*) 12mo. 1641 — Stanbrigii (J.) Vocabularium Metricum, in Latin and English
black letter, *very curious for archaic words* 4to. 1636

146 Vaughan (W.) Directions for Health, Naturall and Artificiall, with two Treatises on the Eyes, 1633—The Schoole of Salernes Regiment of Health, with a necessary Discourse of all Sorts of Fish in use amongst us, black letter, *interspersed with poetry,* 1649

147 Carleton's Tithes Examined, 1606—Epistola ad Regiam Societatem, 1693—Apparatus, *woodcuts,* 1627—Fennor (W.) Compters Commonwealth, or a Voyage to the Infernal Island, *made up with MS.* 1617

148 Shakespeare. Facsimile, made by Netherclift for Mr. J. P. Collier, of the letter of Lord Southampton (H. S.) in which Shakespeare is mentioned *a folio sheet*

149 Collier (J.) Defence of the Short View of the Immorality of the English Stage 1699

150 Jonson (Ben) Fountaine of Self Love, or Cynthia's Revels, as it hath beene sundry times privately acted in the Black Friers by the Children of her Majesties Chappell
first edition 4to. *Imprinted for Walter Burre,* 1601

⁎ There are a few worm-holes, but not into the letter-press, and the bottom of sig. D 4 is slightly cut into one line only, but on the whole it would make a fine copy in the hands of a careful binder. It is, probably, the rarest of all Jonson's separate plays, and very seldom occurs for sale. No copy is cited by Lowndes.

151 Old quarto plays *a parcel*

152 Fletcher (J.) Rule a Wife and Have a Wife, 4to. *Oxford,* 1640 —Massinger's Renegado, acted at the Private Play-house in Drury-lane, *first edition* 1630

153 Rowley (William) New Wonder, a Woman never Vext, a pleasant conceited Comedy, sundry times acted
4to. 1632

154 Rowley (William) Tragedy called All's Lost by Lust, acted by the Lady Elizabeth's Servants
an old prompt copy, marked for acting 4to. 1633

155 Deloney (Thomas) Historie of the Gentle Craft, a most merry and pleasant History, very fit to passe away the tediousness of the long Winter's Evenings
FIRST EDITION, *of extreme rarity, but very imperfect*
Edward White, 1598

156 Kyd (T.) Tragedie of Solimon and Perseda, *reprint of* 1599.

157 Hooper's Reproof to the Rehearsal Transprosed   1673

158 Jordan (Thomas) Money is an Asse, a Comedy as it hath been Acted with good Applause, *one of the scarcest plays of the time of Charles II*   4*to.*   1668

159 Old quarto plays   *a parcel*

160 Chapman (George) Monsieur d'Olive, a Comedie, as it was sundrie times acted by her Majesties Children at the Blacke-friers
     FIRST EDITION   4*to.*   1606

161 Massinger (P.) Maid of Honour
     FIRST EDITION   1632

162 Heywood (J.) Mery Play of Johan Johan, *reprint*, 1533—The Night Walker, or the Little Thief, *MS. title*, 1640—Kempe (A. J.) Loseley Manuscripts, 1836

163 Aristippus, or the Joviall Philosopher, presented in a Private Shew, to which is added the Conceited Pedler
     an unusually large copy   4*to.*   1631

     *** Although this play cannot be considered a rarity, yet it is far from common in a fine clean state like the present copy. Its curiosity, in a literary point of view, we do not remember to have seen noticed. In addition to the allusions to Mulde-Sack, Robin Goodfellow, Taylor the water-poet, Banks' horse, Scoggins' fleas, Skelton, Fennor, &c., there is a ridicule of the prologue of Shakspere's Troilus and Cressida, and at p. 18 is a line which Milton has nearly verbally copied in his poem of l'Allegro.

164 Middleton (T.) Michaelmas Terme, as it hath beene sundry Times Acted by the Children of Paules, newly corrected
     4*to.*   1630

165 Tighe (R. R.) and Davis (J. E.) Annals of Windsor, being a History of the Castle and Town, with some Account of Eton, 2 vol. *plates*   1858

166 Way (A.) Promptorium Parvulorum sive Clericorum, Lexicon Anglo-Latinum Princeps, 2 vol. *with MS. notes and corrections*   4*to.*   Camden Soc. 1843-53

167 Recorde (Robert) Grounde of Artes, teaching the Worke and Practice of Arithmeticke both in Whole numbers and in Fractions
     black letter, *imperfect, but curious from containing a large number of old pen-and-ink comical miniatures*

168 SIR GYLES GOOSECAPPE KNIGHT, a Comedie presented by the Children of the Chappell
     FIRST EDITION, *fine copy*
     4*to.*   *Printed by John Windet for E. Blunt,* 1606

169 Middleton (Thomas) Inner Temple Masque, or Masque of
Heroes, presented as an Entertainment for many worthy
Ladies by Gentlemen of the same ancient and noble house
FIRST EDITION, *fine copy, but the head-line cut into*
4to. *Printed for John Browne,* 1619
*** The present copy, which is the Roxburghe, and sold at
that sale for £2 16s., is the only one cited by Lowndes.

170 Day (John) Ile of Guls, as it hath been often playd in the
Blacke Fryars by the Children of the Revels
FIRST EDITION, *an impression of great rarity, fine copy, but
the last sheet mended*   4to. *John Hodgets,* 1606

171 NERO. The Tragedie of Claudius Tiberius Nero, Rome's
greatest Tyrant, truly represented out of the purest
Records of those Times
FIRST EDITION, *a fine clean copy of an impression almost
always found in bad condition, one edge of dedication
slightly cut*   4to. *Printed for Francis Burton,* 1607

172 Marlowe (C.) Troublesome Raigne and Lamentable Death of
Edward the Second, King of England, with the Tragicall
Fall of Proud Mortimer, 1622—Marlowe (C.) Famous
Tragedy of the Rich Jew of Malta, as it was Play'd at
White-hall and the Cock-pit, 1633
fine copies, morocco, gilt edges   4to. *in 1 vol.*

173 Heywood (Thomas) Golden Age, or the Lives of Jupiter and
Saturne, as it hath beene sundry times acted at the Red
Bull by the Queenes Majesties Servants
large copy, with contemporary MS. notes, very scarce
4to. *Printed for William Barrenger,* 1611

174 Greene (Robert) Spanish Masquerado, wherein under a pleasant devise is discovered effectuallie the pride and inso-
lencie of the Spanish Estate
black letter, *fine copy*   1589
*** Following the dedication to Hugh Ofley, Sheriff of
London, is a sonnet in French by Thomas Lodge.

175 Lilly (John) Dramatic Works, edited by Fairholt, 2 vol. 1858

176 Palsgrave (J.) Dictionarie of Substantives and Adjectives,
English and French, taken from the reprint made by the
French Government   4to. 1530

177 Stephen (H.) World of Wonders, or an Introduction to a
Treatise touching the Conformitie of Ancient and Moderne
Wonders
first and rarest edition   folio. *Edinburgh,* 1608
*** The phraseology of Shakespeare is better illustrated by
this work than by any other book existing.—*Caldecott.*

178 Fletcher (P.) Purple Island, or the Isle of Man, together with
Piscatorie Eclogs
LARGE PAPER, *wanting after p.* 102 *in the latter portion*
4to. *Camb.* 1633

179 Harrison (W.) Historicall Description of the Iland of Britaine, with a briefe rehersall of the nature and qualities of the people of England, and such commodities as are to be found in the same
black letter, *with the index, this curious treatise complete, taken from Holinshed* *folio.* 1586

180 Rowlands (S.) Martin Mark-all, Beadle of Bridewell, his Defence and Answere to the Belman of London, with the long-concealed Originall and Regiment of Rogues, gathered out of the Chronicle of Crackeropes, and the Legend of Lossels (Gordonstoun, £5)
black letter *4to. Printed for John Budge,* 1610

181 Levins (P.) Manipulus Vocabulorum, a Dictionarie of English and Latin Wordes; *a transcript of this very curious rhyming dictionary, remarkable for its large number of archaisms* *folio.* 1570

182 Wirtzung (C.) General Practise of Physicke, conteyning all inward and outward parts of the body, by J. Mosan
black letter *folio. George Bishop,* 1605

183 Mirour for Magistrates, wherein may bee seene Examples passed in this Realme
black letter, *poor copy, last leaf defective*
4to. Henry Marsh, 1587

184 Wodroephe (John) Marrow of the French Tongue, with Phrases, Letters Missive, Sentences, Proverbs, Theames, &c. *a curious book* *folio. R. Meighen,* 1625

185 Butler (S.) Hudibras, ed. Grey, 2 vol. *wants one plate,* 8vo. 1799—Palsgrave (J.) Eclaircissement de la Langue Française, publiés par F. Genin, from ed. 1530, 2 vol. *imperfect,* 4to. Paris, 1852

186 Imperfect Books, viz.: Kelway (Thomas) Astronomical Discourse of the Judgement of Nativities, 1593—Dariot's Astrologicall Judgement of the Starres, 1598—A Rich Storehouse or Treasurie for the Diseased, black letter, 1601—The Secrets of Alexis of Piemont, black letter, 1614—Blundevil's Exercises, with a Plaine Description of Mercator's Globes, and the two Globes lately set forth by M. Molinaxe and Sir Francis Drake in his first Voyage into the Indies, black letter, 1636—Borde (Andrew) Breviarie of Health, wherin doth folow remedies for all maner of Sicknesses and Diseases the which may be in Man or Woman, *plate inserted,* black letter, *Thomas East,* 1575 —Ovid's Metamorphosis, translated by Golding, black letter — Bulwer's Man Transformed, or the Artificiall Changeling, *woodcuts,* 1653

187 Lupton (Thomas) Sivqila, Too good to be true ; omen,—

> Though so at a vewe,
> Yet all that I tolde you,
> Is true, I upholde you ;
> Now cease to aske why,
> For I cannot lye.

Herein is shewed by way of dialogue the wonderfull manners of the people of Mauqsun, with other talke not frivolous

black letter   4to.   H. Bynneman, 1584

188 Tunbridge-Walks, or the Yeoman of Kent, 1703 ; and various other Pamphlets and Plays

189 The Humour of the Age, 1701—Dennis's Liberty Asserted, *scene in Canada,* 1704 ; and various others

190 Dover. Account of Dover Harbour, 1586, seven leaves taken from the *castrated* portion of Holinshed's Chronicle, vol. III—Life of King John, from Holinshed—Wits A, B, C, or a Centurie of Epigrammes, *transcript MS.*

191 Mustapha. The Tragedy of Mustapha

> FIRST EDITION, *very rare, imprint cut into* (Rhodes, £2 2s.)   *N. Butter,* 1609

192 Johnson (R.) Second Part of the Famous Historie of the Seven Champions of Christendome, likewise shewing the Princely Prowes of St. George's three sonnes

> black letter, *fine copy, but wanting a few leaves at the end*   4to.   *Printed for Elizabeth Burbie,* 1608

> *** This second part was published separately, and is of excessive rarity, only one other copy being known. See Collier's Bridgewater Catalogue.

193 Archæologia, vol. XXXVII, both parts   4to.   1857

194 Chaucer's Poems, ed. Bell, vols. I to III, the Canterbury Tales, 1854 — Wright's Songs and Carols, 1856 — Singer's Shakespeare, 1826, vols. II and III—Langtoft's Chronicle, 2 vol. *imperfect, with obsolete words marked in MS.*   1810

195 Halliwell (J. O.) Books of Characters, illustrating the Habits and Manners of Englishmen from the Reign of James I to the Restoration   *thick 4to. Privately printed,* 1857

> *** The impression of this interesting and quaint work was strictly limited to *only twenty-five* copies, each copy attested by the printer.

196 Flecknoe (Richard) Ænigmatical Characters, being rather a new Work than a new Impression of the Old

> *perfect, but a few pages having ink-lines drawn across them*   12mo.   *Printed for the Author,* 1665

> *** An unnoticed impression, differing altogether from that of the same year described by Lowndes and Dr. Bliss.

197 Hartlib (S.) Legacy of Husbandry   4*to.*   1655

198 Mastive (The) or Young Whelpe of the Olde Dogge, Epigrams and Satyrs, *woodcut on title, the printed portion of the letter-press title and two leaves supplied in facsimile morocco, gilt edges*   *Tho. Creede,* 1615

*** Published anonymously, but the piece is attributed to HENRY PARROT, respecting whom see Wood's Athenæ, Beloe's Anecdotes, &c. &c. The present copy was priced in the Bibliotheca Anglo-Poetica at £30. It is remarkable for numerous jocose allusions to the manners and customs of the time.

199 Nares (R.) Glossary of Words, Phrases, Customs, Proverbs, &c., illustrating English authors, particularly Shakespeare   4*to.*   1822

200 Machyn (H.) Diary, ed. J. G. Nichols 4*to.*   *Camd. Soc.* 1848

201 Richard the Second. Original Text of the contemporary French metrical history of Richard II, from Harl. MS., from the Archæologia, *two copies*   4*to.*

202 Rymer's Short View of Tragedy, with some Reflections on Shakespeare and other Practitioners for the Stage, *the earliest Shaksperian criticisms, two copies*   8*vo.* 1693

203 Pageant. Relation de ce qui s'est passé a la Haye au mois de Fevrier, 1638, les Festins, Comedies, Bals, &c., au Mariage de Monsieur de Brederode   *very scarce, fine copy uncut*   *fol.* 1638

204 Emblems. Typus Mundi in quo ejus Calamitates et Pericula necnon Divini humanique Amoris antipathia emblematicè proponuntur,   12*mo.*   *Antw.* 1652

*** This curious collection contains the engraving of the ancient game of Troll-my-dames, referred to by Shakespeare.

205 Mary, Queen of Scots. Het Leeven van Maria Stuart, Koninginne van Schotlant   *fine copy, uncut*   4*to.*   *Amst.* 1647

206 Fenner (Dudley) Artes of Logike and Rhetorike, plainely set foorth in the Englishe toonge, easie to be learned and practised, with examples for the practise of the same in the government of the familie   *perfect, but a small corner off one leaf torn*   4*to.*   *No printer's name,* 1584

207 Lodge (Thomas) Paradoxes against common Opinion, debated in form of Declamations in place of publique censure, onelie to exercise yoong wittes in difficult matters   4*to.*   *London, Printed for Simon Waterson,* 1602

*** This piece was published anonymously, but there is little doubt of its authorship, and the present copy has a Latin

3

motto and the initials T. L. in Lodge's neat autograp...
Compare the facsimile of Lodge's signature in the
Shakespeare Society's reprint of the Defence of Poetry,
introd. p. 76. This tract is undescribed by bibliographers, and is probably unique, but it is unfortunately
imperfect.

208 Hexham (Henry) Journael ofte een ware ende kort verhael
van't vermaerde Belegh van de Stadt Breda, 4*to. Delft*, 1638
—Venus Minne-spel ende Cupidoos Boevery, *in verse*, 1647
—Laud (Archbishop) Een Oratie op de Censure van
Johan Bastwick, Henrick Burton, en Willem Prin
4*to. Delff*, 1638

209 Powell (T.) Tom of All Trades, or the Plaine Pathway to Pre-
ferment, found out amongst the inchanted Islands of ill
Fortune, *last leaf MS*. 1631—Decker (Thomas) English
Villanies, Lanthorne and Candle Light, and O per se O
𝔟𝔩𝔞𝔠𝔨 𝔩𝔢𝔱𝔱𝔢𝔯, *imperfect* 1632

210 HEYNS (Zacharias) CONST-THONENDE JUWEEL (the Jewel of
Dramatic Art), published by the Honourable City of
Haerlem in XII Emblematic Plays or Moralities, with
Prologues and Songs arranged according to the regula-
tions of the City Authorities, *numerous plates of Theatrical
Figures and costumes*
a remarkably fine copy, with all the plates
4*to. Zwol*. 1607

*** This copy has also the additional play of Haerlems
Juweel, with plates, separately published in the following year, 1608.

211 Abel and Kilvert. Een t' Samen-spraeck ofte voorghevalle
Discours tuffchen Mr. Alderman Abel ende Richard
Kilvert, *curious woodcut* 4*to*. 1641

212 Old Parr. Wonderlijcke Afbeeldinge van een Seer Oude Man,
genaemt Thomas Parr, welcke out gheworden is over de
152 Jaren, en heeft geleeft tot anno 1635, *a broadside,
with an engraving of Thomas Parr*.

213 Laud (Archbishop) De Oratie ofte Verklaringhe van John
Pym esquire teghens William Laud, *with a remarkably
fine impression of a portrait of Laud, engraved by
Visscher* *Amst*. 1641

214 Notices of Early Editions of Shakespeare, by J. O. Halliwell,
pp. 14, 8vo., *the remainder out of twenty-five copies only
printed, ten copies* 1857

215 Greene's Dorastus and Fawnia,
𝔟𝔩𝔞𝔠𝔨 𝔩𝔢𝔱𝔱𝔢𝔯, a large fragment of a very early edition

216 HULOET (RICHARD) ABCEDARIUM ANGLICO-LATINUM, pro
Tyrunculis, Ricardo Huloeto Enscriptore
FIRST EDITION, *fine copy*   *fol. Riddell,* 1552
  *** This first edition is, next to the Promptorium Parvulorum,
the most valuable early English dictionary known to
philologists. The second and only other edition, issued
in 1572, is so modernised and altered as to be almost
another work

217 Shakespeare. Title-page of the first folio edition of Shakespeare's Works, 1623, with the portrait, an admirably executed facsimile by Harris

218 Theobald's Shakespeare, portrait and plates, 8 vols., *one or
two of the volumes are mutilated*   8vo. 1752

219 Bradshaw's Ghost, 1659—One and Thirty New Orders of
Parliament, and the Parliament's Ghost, to the tune of
Mad Tom, 1659—Your Servant, Gentlemen, or what
think you of a query, 1659—The Red Coat's Catechisme,
1659—The Life and approaching Death of W. Kiffin,
1659; and various other pamphlets

220 Newcastle. Pye (John) True and Perfect Account of a
Strange and Dreadful Apparition, which lately infested
and sunk a ship bound for Newcastle   4*to.* 1672

221 Guthrey (James) True and Perfect Speech as it was delivered
by himself immediately before his Execution at Edin-
brough   4*to.* 1661

222 D. (R.) True Relation of his Adventures in Affrica, Arabia,
with a true Description of a City near the mountain
Gubell   4*to.* 1672

223 London. True Relation of the Dispute and Bloody Conflict
between the Spaniards and the French at Tower-Wharfe
and Tower-Hill, September, 1661.—A Conference held in
the Tower of London between two Aldermen of the City,
1660—Saint Paul's Potion prescribed by Doctors Com-
mons, *curious*, 1641—Baron Tomlinson's Speech to the
Sheriffs of London, 1659—The Outcry of the London
Prentices, 1659   4*to.*

224 Tracts relating to Hugh Peters, viz., Peters's Resurrection by
way of Dialogue between him and a Merchant, 1659.—
A Conference held between the old Lord Protector and
the new Lord General, truly reported by Hugh Peters,
1660—Oliver Cromwell's Thanks faithfully presented by
Hugh Peters, *in prose and verse*, n.d.   4*to.*

225 Cheshire. One and Twenty Chester Queries, 1659—A Dialogue betwixt Sir George Booth and Sir John Presbyter
at their meeting near Chester   4*to.* 1659

_13_ 226 Gainsford (T.) Glory of England, or a true Description
many excellent prerogatives and remarkable blessings,
whereby she triumpheth over all the Nations in the
world   4to.   Printed by Edw. Griffin, 1620
₊ This is an undescribed edition of a curious work, which
contains many interesting and amusing allusions.

/-2-6 227 HOLINSHED (RALPH) CHRONICLES of England, Ireland, and
Scotland, by Hooker, with the castrations, 4 vol.
BEST EDITION, black letter, fine copy, old calf gilt
                                    fol.   1588

/-/-0 228 Napier (Baron, of Merchistoun) Description of the Admirable
Table of Logarithmes, invented by that honourable Lord
John Nepair, Baron of Marchiston, translated by E.
Wright, with preface by Henry Briggs, dedicated to the
East India Company, with verses by Davies of Hereford
and R. Lever
very scarce   8vo.   Printed for Simon Waterson, 1618

_2_ 229 Montelyon Knight of the Oracle
black letter, wanting title and a few leaves, 4to. circa 1600
₊ This edition is earlier by many years than any other known,
a fact ascertained not merely by the character of the type,
but by the antique language and orthography, which
differ considerably from those of later impressions.

_/_ 230 Durfey (T.) Tales Tragical and Comical, 1704—A True and
Exact Relation of the Strange Finding Out of Moses his
Tombe, defective at end, 1657

_6_ 231 Moore (Sir Jonas) Mathematical Compendium, or Useful
Practices in Arithmetick, &c., by N. Stephenson, unnoticed by Prof. De Morgan   12mo.   1674

/-5-0 232 Skeffington (Sir John) Heroe of Lorenzo, or the Way to
Eminence and Perfection, with address to the reader by
Isaac Walton, fine copy   12mo.   1652

_₊6_ 233 S. (W.) Instructions for the increasing of Mulberie Trees, and
the breeding of Silke-Wormes, woodcuts, poor copy,
1609—The Art of Limning, which teacheth the order in
drawing and tracing of letters, vinets, flowers, &c., black
letter, four last leaves torn, 1583   4to. in 1 vol.

_₊/_ 234 Primaudaye (P. de la) French Academie, wherein is discoursed
the Institution of Maners
FIRST EDITION   4to.   1586
₊ This first edition is of great rarity.   See Collier's Poetical
Decameron, vol. II, p. 275.

_6_ 235 London.   A Submissive Address and Humble Petition of the
poor decayed Freemen and Widows now Prisoners in
Ludgate, near 200 souls, and daily increasing, against this
time of Whitsontide, 1677, woodcut, a small broadside
extremely curious   Printed by E. F. 1677

236 Deptford, Greenwich, Woolwich, &c. True Relation of the great and terrible Inundation of Waters and Overflowing of the Lower Town of Deptford, Greenwich, &c. *woodcut fine copy* 4to. *Imprinted for George Horton*, 1651

237 America. Mr. Baxter Baptiz'd in Bloud, or a sad History of the unparall'd Cruelty of the Anabaptists in New England, faithfully relating the Cruel, Barbarous, and Bloudy Murther of Mr. Baxter, an orthodox Minister, who was kill'd by the Anabaptists, and his Skin most cruelly flead off from his body, with an exact account of all the circumstances and particularities of this barbarous Murther. Published by his mournfull brother, Benjamin Baxter, living in Fenchurch Street, London
4to. *Printed in the year* 1673.

238 Rich (Barnaby) New Description of Ireland, wherein is described the Disposition of the Irish whereunto they are inclined, *four leaves MS.*
scarce (Sykes, £5) 4to. *Thomas Adams*, 1610

239 London. The London Chaunticleres, a witty Comœdy, full of Various and Delightfull Mirth, often acted with great Applause
a very scarce and curious play, the characters being London criers 4to. 1659

240 Heinsius (D.) Laus Pediculi, or an Apologeticall Speech, directed to the Worshipfull Masters and Wardens of Beggars Hall
very rare, but query title doctored or in facsimile
Thomas Harper, 1634

241 Botero (G.) Treatise Concerning the Causes of the Magnificence and Greatnes of Cities, in three Bookes, by R. Peterson 4to. *R. Ockould*, 1606

242 Smith (Richard) Trial of Trueth, or a Treatise wherein is declared who should be Judge betweene the Reformed Churches and the Romists
black letter 4to. *Robert Dexter*, 1591

243 London. Sermon at the Election of the Lord Mayor, by A. Burgesse, 1644—Sermons earnestly enveying against the Sins of this land, *and in particular against the Sins of this City of London*, 1615—Declaration concerning his Majesties advancing with his Army toward London, 1642 —God's Appearing, preached at St. Paul's, 1655—The Two Witnesses, Sermons preached at Lawrence Jewry, 1643 5 *vo.*

244 Massinger (P.) Bondman, FIRST EDITION, *large copy*, 4to. 1638—Wars in Germanie, with the True Relation of the Taking of the Towne of Aix, 1614—Discolliminium, *a curious tract for odd vernacular phraseology*, 1650—A Sermon Preached at Bristol, 1685 4 *vol.*

_/_ 245 Johnston (J.) Inscriptiones Historicæ Regum Scotorum, Jo— —
Jonstono Abredonense Scoto Authore, *title MS, u...
otherwise imperfect*   4to. *Amstd.* 1602

_3 /1_ 246 Cabinet of Mirth, or Comic Medley, *front. n. d.*—Life of
Matthew Lee, executed at Tyburn, 1752, *Bristol,* 1770—
Merlin's Life and Prophecies, *view of Richmond Park,*
1755   3 *vol.*

_3 - 10 0_ 247 L. (L.) OWLES ALMANACKE, prognosticating many strange
accidents which shall happen to this Kingdome of Great
Britaine this year, 1618, found in an Ivy-bush, and now
published by Mr. Jocundary Merrie-braines, *large woodcut*
       4to.   1618

    ** A facetious book, replete with curious allusions to the
manners and customs of the time.

_— /9 —_ 248 Jacke Drum's Entertainement, or the Comedie of Pasquil and
Katherine, as it hath beene sundry times plaid by the
Children of Powles
fine copy   4to.   1616

_— /5_ 249 Day (John) Humour Out of Breath, a Comedie divers times
latelie acted by the Children of the Kings Revells
rare   1608

_1 - 10. 0_ 250 Chapman (G.) Gentleman Usher, FIRST EDITION   1606

_1 - 19 - 0_ 251 Breton (N.) Post with a Packet of Mad Letters, newly imprinted, *both parts*
   black letter, *wants half-title to the second part, woodcut*
       4to. *Printed by E. Okes,* 1669

    ** An extraordinarily fine copy, uncut edges throughout,
and in beautiful condition. The title is in so clean a state,
it was returned from Dr. Bliss's sale as a reprint; but
there can, we think, be no doubt of its genuineness.

_— .3 h_ 252 Coles (E.) English Dictionary, 1685—Earle's Microcos-
mography, ed. Bliss, 1811   8vo.   2 *vol.*

_— /5 —_ 253 ROMEO AND JULIET. Historias Tragicas Exemplares sacadas _BARTON_.
de las obras del Bandello Verones (*Historia tercera, de
Romeo y Julieta*)
fine copy, extremely rare   8vo. *Salamanca,* 1589

_— 4 h_ 254 Walker on Shakespeare's Versification, 8vo. 1854—Hudson's
Shakespeare, 1851, vols. II and III—Singer's Shakespeare,
1856, vols. I and II

_— /0 —_ 255 Adam in Eden or Nature's Paradise, by William Coles,
herbarist, *fol.* 1657—Bullein's Bulwarke of Defence, Book
of Simples, Dialogue between Soarenesse and Chirurgy,
black letter, *woodcuts, wants a few leaves, fol. Imprinted
by Thomas Marshe,* 1579   2 *vol.*

256 Tusser (Thomas) Five Hundred Points of Good Husbandry, as well for the Champion or open Countrey, as also for the Woodland or Severall

    black letter, *large copy*   *4to.* 1638

257 Shakespeare (W.) King John, reprint of first folio, pp. 3 to 22, with MS. notes and collations—Hayward's Henry the Fourth, *4to.* 1599—Lucius Junius Brutus, 1681—A Poem upon Tea, 1712—Generall Demands propounded at Aberdeen, *imperfect*, 1638—Early Alterations in the Text of Shakespeare's Plays, pp. 12, *inedited MS.*—Kean's edition of the Winter's Tale, 1856—Troublesome Raigne of King John, from the Miscellaneous Pieces of English Poesie, 1764—Cowley's Poems, preface only, noticing Shakespeare, 1656

258 Reeves (W.) Apologies of Justin Martyr, Tertullian, and Minutius Felix, in defence of the Christian Religion, 2 *vol.*   *8vo.* 1709

259 Tertullian's Works, vol. I, *all published, Oxford,* 1842—Giles' Heathen Records, 1856—Tatiani Oratio ad Græcos (from Otto's Corpus Apol. Christ. vol. VI), 1851—Bullet's History of Christianity, 1776—Phlegon Re-examined, 1735   5 *vol. 8vo.*

260 Origen against Celsus, translated from the Original into English by James Bellamy, Gent.

    both parts, fine copy   *8vo. n. d.*

261 Holinshed's Second Volume of Chronicles, black letter, *imperfect*, 1586, and four large fragments of Holinshed, ed. 1587—Peck's Desiderata Curiosa, vol. I, *port.*, 1732, *wants list of contents*—Catalogue of Malone's Library, *imperfect, but with MS. notes and numerous MS. references to other copies of books in the British Museum*, 1836

262 Book of Rates, 1675—Cockeram's English Dictionarie, *one leaf defective, a rare edition*, 1626—Fulwood's Castell of Memorie, black letter, 1573, *wants title and one leaf*—Bacon (Sir F.) Wisedome of the Ancients, 1619—Wither (G.) Abuses Stript and Whipt, Epithalamia or Nuptiall Poems, Faire Virtue, the Mistresse of Philarete, *imperfect*, 1633—Rules of Civility, or Certain Ways of Deportment observed amongst Persons of Quality, *leaf of contents wanting*, 1685—Ray (J.) English Words, *the earliest work on English Provincialisms*, a fine copy, but small corner of p. 173 torn, 1674—Kelly's Scottish Proverbs, *imperfect*

263 Markham (Gervase) Hunger's Prevention, or the whole Arte of Fowling by Water and Land

    FIRST EDITION, *ded. to Sir E. Sands, and Thomas Gibbs, Esq., woodcuts*   1621

264 B. (J.) Epitome of the Art of Husbandry, with Directions
the use of the Angle, and the New Additions, 1675—
Mun's English Treasure by Forraign Trade, *the first book
on free trade*, 1664—The French Schoole-Master, newly
corrected and enlarged with several quaint Proverbs,
1649—Weldon's Court and Character of King James,
1651

265 Massinger (P.) Fatall Dowry, 1632—Chapman (G.) Ball, a
Comedy, 1639—An Excellent Tragedy of Mulleasses
the Turke, and Borgias Governour of Florence, full of
interchangeable variety beyond expectation, *scarce*, 1632

266 GRUB-STREET. The Picture of the Observator (John Tutchin)
drawn to the life, *with large woodcut of Tutchin in the
pillory, superscribed,* " In 1685 I was convicted in the
West, to be whipp'd in every market town once a year,
but now I find I must stand here," 1704—T—ch—n
(Tutchin) Touch'd to the Quick, or Factions Secretary
Whipp'd at the Cartsarse, *large woodcut*—Daniel de Foe
and the Devil at Leap-frog, being a Dialogue which pass'd
between them, as they were recreating themselves at that
Sport in an Eminent Tavern in Cheapside, *large woodcut
of the devil, De Foe, and Pinkethman*, 1706—Smith-
field Groans, or the horrid Wickedness committed
and conniv'd at in Bartholomew Fair, *in verse*, 1707—
The Seven Extinguishers, 1710—A Trip to Kensington, or
that Town drawn to the Life, *in verse*, 1710—A Catalogue
of Petitioners in the Long Parliament, from Mr.
William Prinn, 1699—Paul Dick, or the Chat of the
Gods at their Tea-table—A Search after Knavery, or a
Visitation of the Bakers, *woodcut of two in the pillory*,
1693—A Description of Scotland and its Inhabitants,
1705—The New Socket-money Tax upon all degrees of
marriage, *a piece of ribaldry*, 1694—The New West-
minster Wedding or the Rampant Vicar, licens'd 1693,
printed for the inhabitants of Ipswich—The Famous Will
of Madam Dorothy Fish, a maiden Gentlewoman, aged
Sixty Three, late of the Parish of Hackney, *head-line cut
into*—The London Virgin's Vindication in a Letter from a
Young Lady of the Play-house, to the Executors of Mrs.
Dorothy Fish, late School-mistress at Hackney, *dated in
MS.*1694—Proposals for Printing Emblems concerning
the Secrets of Nature, *plates*—Hocus Pocus, call'd the
French King to Life again, or Old Nick blew Wind, &c.,
woodcut, 1705—The Proceedings at the Tryal, Examina-
tion and Condemnation of a certain Scribling, Rhyming,
Versifying, Poeteering Hosier, and True-born English-
man, commonly known by the name of Daniel the
Prophet, *alias* Anglipoliski, *alias* Foeski, *alias* your

humble Servant De F. 1705, in 1 vol. *an exceedingly
curious collection of fugitive pieces, chiefly those printed
with half titles on two leaves only, with dates, prices, and
suppressed names by the original Collector* 4to.

*** "A curious Collection of Grub-street," MS. note by J.
Bindley, 1787. It may be worth notice that, in the tract
respecting Dorothy Fish, the will of that lady, dated
1694, is witnessed by Jonson, Fletcher, Massinger,
Shirley, *and Shakespeare!*

267 Shakespeare. The Fairy Queen, an Opera represented at the
Queen's Theatre by their Majesties Servants (altered from
A Midsummer Night's Dream) *with the preface, some-
times wanting* 4to. 1692

268 Wilkes' General View of the Stage (including Criticisms on
Shakespeare), 1759—Gilchrist (O.) Examination of the
Charges of Ben Jonson's Enmity to Shakespeare, 1808—
The Rape of Lucrece, written by Mr. William Shakespeare,
and Venus and Adonis, *from Poems on Affairs of State,*
1707 8vo.

269 Shakespeare (W.) Winter's Tale, reprint from the first folio
edition, *interleaved, with MS. collations* folio

270 Shakespeare. Henry the Fourth, with the Humours of Sir
John Falstaff, revived with Alterations
very scarce 4to. 1700

271 Zouch (R.) Sophister, a Comedy, 1639—Hide Parke, a Comedie,
1637—Heywood (Thomas) Wise Woman of Hogsdon, a
Comedie, *very rare, but title and one leaf MS.* 1638—
Jonson (Ben) Catiline, his Conspiracy, 1635—The City
Night-Cap, or, *Crede quod habes et habes, scarce* 1661

272 Goffe (Thomas) Couragious Turke, or Amurath the First, a
Tragedie
FIRST EDITION 4to. 1632

*** Perhaps the most bombastic play in the English language.
The hero, addressing the stars, asks,—"Why put you on
those periwigs of fire!"

273 Rowley (Samuel) Noble Souldier, or a Contract Broken justly
Reveng'd, a Tragedy 4to. 1634

274 Shirley (J.) Humorous Courtier, 1640—Shirley (J.) Constant
Maid, 1640—Davenant (W.) Witts, a Comedie presented
at the Private House in Blacke Fryers, 1636—Jonson,
Fletcher, and Middleton's Widdow, a Comedie, FIRST
EDITION, *head line cut into,* 1652—The Tragedy of Nero
newly written, 1633—The Fatal Contract, a French
Tragedy, 1653—The Rivall Friends, a Comœdie acted
before the King at Cambridge, March, 1631, cryed downe
by Boyes, Faction, Envie, and Confident Ignorance, 1632

4

—The Duke's Mistris, 1638—The Conspiracy, as it was intended for the Nuptialls of the Lord Charles Herbert and the Lady Villiers, *large copy*, 1638—Shirley (H.) Martyr'd Souldier, 1638—The Dumbe Knight, an Historicall Comedy, *two slight defects*, 1633—The Combat of Love and Friendship, 1654

275 Ford (J.) Lovers Melancholy, acted at the Private House in the Blacke Friers, and publikely at the Globe by the Kings Majesties Servants

FIRST EDITION, *with MS. additions and alterations, some pasted down over the text, others insertions, apparently for acting*   1629

276 Il Sacrificio Comedia de gli Ingannati celebrato ne i Giuochi di uno Carnevale in Siena (*origin of Twelfth Night*)

Venet. 1609

277 Lacey (J.) Sauny the Scott, or the Taming of the Shrew (altered from Shakespeare)

FIRST EDITION, *very scarce*   4*to.*   1698

278 Beaumont and Fletcher's Wild Goose Chace, *wormed, a remarkably fine copy, probably large paper*, 1652—Proverbes, English and French, from Howell's Tetraglotton, 1660—Parkinson's Paradisus Terrestris, a Garden of all Sorts of Pleasant Flowers, *one or two slight defects, and imperfect indices*, 1629—Browne's Pseudodoxia Epidemica, 1646—Sandys (G.) Relation of a Journey begun 1610, *woodcuts*, 1615—Sydney (Sir P.) Arcadia, *imperfect, but with very early MS. notes*

279 Shakespeare. The Waking Man's Dreame, a fragment from a *BARTH* book printed about 1630   4*to.*

⁎ This fragment contains the whole of the story, which is that of the Induction to the Taming of the Shrew. It is supposed to be a reprint of the lost story-book of Edwards. See the Papers of the Shakespeare Society.

280 Jonson (Ben) Every Man in his Humour, as it hath beene sundry times publickly acted by the Right Honorable the Lord Chamberlaine his Servants

FIRST EDITION, *very rare* (Bindley, £1 14*s.*) *wormed*
Imprinted for Walter Burre, 1601

281 Microcosmus, a Morall Maske presented with generall liking at the private House in Salisbury Court, 1637—The Chronicle Historie of Perkin Warbeck, a strange Truth, 1634—The Schoole of Complement, 1631—Wit without Money, a Comedie, 1639—Heywood (T.) and Rowley (W.) Fortune by Land and Sea, *a scarce play, but some of the letter-press cut into*, 1655—May (T.) Old Couple, a Comedy, 1658—Shirley's Politician, 1655

282 Blundevil (Thomas) Art of Riding, Dieting of Horses, and Order of Curing Horse-diseases
blackletter 4to. 1580

283 Gildon (C.) Reflections on Mr. Rymer's Short View of Tragedy, and an Attempt at a Vindication of Shakespeare, *from Gildon's Miscellaneous Letters* 8vo. 1694

284 Wheler (R. B.) Historical and Descriptive Account of the Birth-Place of Shakespeare, with lithographic Illustrations by C. F. Green
scarce 4to. *Stratford-on-Avon*, 1824

285 Defoe (D.) Vie et les Avantures surprenantes de Robinson Crusoe, *plates*
an early and rare foreign translation of this popular work
8vo. *Amst.* 1720

286 Shakespeare. A Hand-List of Books, Manuscripts, &c. illustrative of the Life and Writings of Shakespeare, collected between the years 1842 and 1859, by J. O. Halliwell, Esq. 8vo. *Only 30 copies privately printed*, 1859.
** This collection contains upwards of three hundred volumes, entirely relating to Shakespeare.

287 —— Another copy.

288 Shadwell (Thomas) History of Timon of Athens, the Man-Hater, as it is acted at the Dukes Theatre, *first edition*, 1678—Macbeth, a Tragædy, with all the Alterations, &c. and New Songs, 1674

289 Bradwell (T.) Watchman for the Pest, teaching the true Rules of Preservation from the Pestilent Contagion at this time fearfully overflowing this famous Cittie of London
4to. 1625

290 Shakespeare (W.) Julius Cæsar, a Tragedy, as it is now acted at the Theatre Royal 4to. 1684

291 Middleton (Thomas) Two New Playes, viz.: More Dissemblers besides Women, and Women beware Women
scarce *Humphrey Moseley*, 1657

292 Ritson (J.) Cursory Criticisms on the Edition of Shakspeare published by Edmond Malone
scarce 8vo. 1792

293 Heywood (J.) Mery Play of Johan Johan, 1533, *reprint*—Wright's Songs and Carols, *Warton Club*, 1856—Cock Lorelles Bote, *Percy Soc.* 1843—Westward for Smelts, *Percy Soc.* 1848—Manifest Detection of Dice Play, *Percy Soc.* 1850—Pleasant Conceits of Old Hobson, *Percy Soc.* 1843—Deloney's Strange Histories, *Percy Soc.* 1841—The Interlude of the Trial of Treasure, *Percy Soc.* 1850

294 Royal Society. Philosophical Transactions, parts 2 and 3 for 1856, parts 1, 2, and 3 for 1857, and part 1 for 1858
6 *parts*, 4to.

295 Shakespeare (William) Two Parts of Henry the Fourth, from the reprint of ed. 1623, *interleaved, with numerous MS. collations, and a few MS. notes* *folio*

296 Shakespeare (William) Antony and Cleopatra, from reprint of the first folio, *interleaved, with numerous collations*—Life and Death of Richard the Second, p. 23 to p. 44, from the same edition, *with MS. collations*—Othello, p. 310 to p. 338, from the same edition, *with MS. collations*

297 Shakespeare (W.) Hamlet, 1603. Diminutive photograph from the copy wanting the title, but having the last leaf UNIQUE, *being the only copy preserved*

*** Great pains were taken with this photograph, but, owing to the discoloration of the original paper, some of the pages are indistinct. It is believed to be a complete copy, save the title, but will be sold not subject to collation.

298 Tate (N.) History of King Richard the Second, acted at the Theatre Royal under the Name of the Sicilian Usurper, *altered from Shakespeare*
scarce *4to.* 1681

299 Shakespeare. A Word or Two of Advice to William Warburton, a Dealer in many Words, by a Friend, with an Appendix containing a taste of William's Spirit of Railing
extremely scarce 1746

300 Daniel (S.) Delia and Rosamond augmented, with the Tragedie of Cleopatra, *first title wanting, and otherwise defective* 16mo. *Printed by Peter Short for Simon Waterson,* 1598

*** An *unique* edition, unnoticed by all bibliographers.

301 Mucedorus. A Most Pleasant Comedie of Mucedorus, the King's Sonne of Valencia, and Amadine, the King's Daughter of Aragon, with the Merry Conceits of Mouse, very delectable and full of conceited Mirth, *attributed by some to Shakespeare*
4to. Imprinted at London for William Jones, 1613

302 Shakespeare (W. *attributed to*) Merry Divel of Edmonton, as it hath beene sundry times Acted by his Majesties Servants at the Globe on the Banke Side
SECOND EDITION, *fine copy, very rare*
4to. Printed by G. Eld for Arthur Johnson, 1617

*** The third edition is the earliest cited by Lowndes as sold in sales.

303 Middleton (T.) Tragi-Coomodie called the Witch, long since acted at the Blackfriers
privately printed, uncut 1778

304 Rimbault (E. F.) Nursery Rhymes, with the Tunes to which they are still Sung, *4to.*—Wright (T.) Narratives of Sorcery and Magic, 2 vol. 8vo. 1851—Soane (G.) New Curiosities of Literature, 2 vol. 8vo. 1849

1 Shakespeare (W.) Tragical History of Richard the Third, altered by Cibber, *plate*, 1745—Julius Cæsar, a Tragedy, *plate*, 1741 ; and others *in 1 vol.*

*10*306 Savile (Thomas) Raising of Them that are Fallen, a Discourse very Profitable, *with verses at the end*
a very rare book 4to. *Printed for William Welby*,1606

— *2* 307 Chateaubriand (F. A.) Travels, 2 vol. 8vo. 1812

*17*308 Shakespeare. Galerie des Femmes de Shakespeare, collection de Quarante-cinq Portraits 8vo. *Paris, n. d.*

309 Davies (John) Microcosmos, the Discovery of the Little World,
4-2-0 with the government thereof, *with the unpaged leaves at the end* 4to. *Oxford*, 1603

   ⁎ See at page 215 the curious and interesting allusions to Shakespeare and Burbage, as actors, and their initials in the margin.

*3-0-0*310 Silvayn (Alexander) Orator, handling a hundred severall Discourses in forme of Declamations, some of the Arguments being drawne from Titus Livius and other ancient Writers, the rest of the Author's own Invention ; part of which are of matters happened in our Age, Englished by L. Piot (Munday)
fine copy 4to. *Printed by Adam Islip*, 1596

   ⁎ This interesting collection of tales includes at p. 400 the story of Shakespeare's Merchant of Venice, "Of a Jew who would for his debt have a pound of the flesh of a Christian." In a previous sale, a copy sold for £7 12s.

311 Saviolo (Vincentio) his Practise in two Bookes, the first in-
4-0-0 treating of the Use of the Rapier and Dagger, the second of Honor and Honorable Quarrels, *both parts, curious woodcuts*
FINE COPY, *morocco, gilt edges, by Bedford*
4to. *Printed by John Wolfe*, 1595

   ⁎ This work is generally believed, and with good reason, to be alluded to by Shakespeare in As You Like It. It is very illustrative of allusions both in Shakespeare and Ben Jonson. As originally published, it contained eleven leaves less than in the present copy. Afterwards, the first leaf of sheet I was cancelled, and twelve additional leaves inserted in its place, forming the complete book as in this copy. The second leaf of sheet I is erroneously marked H 2. In some copies, both the cancelled leaf and the additional sheet occur, but the former is certainly out of place, being repeated. There are, therefore, three different kinds of copies, all virtually perfect.

312 W. (W.) New and Merrie Prognostication, devised on
the finest fashion—

Made and written for this present yeare,
By foure witty Doctors, as shall appeare,
Spendall, Whoball, and Doctor Dews-ace,
With them Will Sommer takes his place;
They have consulted all in deede,
To solace them that this shall reede.

in verse, woodcuts, FINE COPY

4to. *Printed by Edward Allde, and are to be sold by
John Tapp at his Shop at St. Magnus Corner,* 1623

** Only one other copy of this somewhat coarse, but curious,
poem, is known to exist.

313 Rich (Barnaby) True and Kinde Excuse written in Defence of
that Booke intituled A Newe Description of Irelande,
pleasant and pleasing both to English and Irish
fine copy, very scarce 4to. 1612

314 Rich (Barnaby) Catholicke Conference betweene Syr Tady
Mac Mareall, a popish priest of Waterforde, and Patricke
Plaine, a young Student in Trinity College by Dublin in
Ireland, strange to be related, credible to be beleeved, and
pleasant to bee perused
fine copy, very scarce 4to. 1612

315 Ben Jonson. Wit's Academy, or Six Penyworth for a Peny,
being Ben Johnson's last Arrow to all Citizen's Wives and
London Dames, shot from his famous poetical Quiver, to
the general view of the courteous Reader, laid open by
way of Question and Answer, and interlarded with sundry
choice Conceits upon the Times, very pleasant and delightful

morocco, gilt edges, by Bedford.

4to. *Imprinted at London by R. Wood,* 1656

** A very curious piece, believed to be unique.

316 Pantagruel's Prognostication, certain, true, and infallible,
newly compos'd for the benefit and instruction of hair-
brain'd and idle Fellowes, by Mr. Alcofribas, Sewer in
Chief to Pantagruel, set forth long since by Francis
Rabelais, done in the way and by the Tables of an
Astrologer of the first Magnitude, and now translated by
Democritus Pseudomantis, *imprint cut off*

a fine, sound, clean copy, morocco 12mo.

** This early and curious chap-book is believed to be unique.
It is preceded by a dedication to William Lilly, and a
Skeltonical poem, entitled, 'Skelton upon Rabelais.''

317 Machiavel. The Uncasing of Machivil's Instructions to his
Sonne, with the Answere to the same, *in verse*
very rare, morocco, gilt edges, by Bedford
4to. *Printed for Thomas Bushell,* 1613

HEYWOOD (THOMAS) IF YOU KNOW NOT ME, you know Nobodie,
or the Troubles of Queene Elizabeth, *woodcut*
FIRST EDITION, *fine copy, morocco, gilt edges, by Bedford*
4to. Printed for Nathaniel Butter, 1605

*** This was published a year before the date of any edition
recorded by bibliographers. Only one other copy of it is
known.

319 Twyne (T.) Shorte and Pithie Discourse concerning the en-
gendring, tokens, and effects of all Earthquakes in
Generall, particularly that within the Citie of London,
which hapned upon Wensday in Easter Weeke last Past,
the Sixt day of April, almost at six a clocke in the evening,
woodcut, black letter, *morocco by Bedford, extremely
rare*   *4to. Printed by Richarde Johnes,* 1580

320 KNIGHT OF THE SEA. The Heroicall Adventures of the Knight
of the Sea, comprised in the most famous and renowned
Historie of the illustrious and excellently accomplished
Prince Oceander, Grand-sonne to the mightie and mag-
nanimous Claranax, Emperour of Constantinople, and the
Empresse Basilia, and sonne unto the incomparable
Olbiocles, Prince of Grecia, by the beautious Princesse
Almidiana, daughter unto the puissant King Rubaldo of
Hungaria ; wherein is described his parents misfortunes
and captivities, his owne losse, strange preserving, education, and fostering by Kanyra Queen of Carthage, his
Knighthood, admirable exploytes, and unmatchable at-
chievementes, graced with the most glorious conquestes
over knights, gyants, monsters, enchauntments, realmes,
and dominions ; with his fortunate comming to the
knowledge of his parents in the greatest extreamitie of
their captivitie ; his combating, affecting, and pursuites in
his love towardes the rarely embellished Princesse and
lady-knight Phianora, daughter unto the invincible
Argamont, King of England, by the gracious Princesse
Clarecinda
black letter, *prose intermixed with verse,* pp. 239, *morocco, gilt
edges, by Bedford   4to. Printed for William Leake,* 1600

*** One of the rarest and most curious English romances
known, the only other copy being that which sold at the
Roxburgh sale for £25. It is a mock romance, written
with the intention of ridiculing the tales of giants,
magicians, and dragons, and contains a vast number of
curious allusions. The present copy is substantially
perfect, but it wants part of a leaf at sig. C 3, and one or
two very slight defects. The name of the author is not
known. On the last leaf are some verses by one R. W.

321 Shakespeare (W.) First and Second Part of the Troublesome Raigne of John King of England, with the Discoverie King Richard's base Sonne, also the death of King John at Swinstead Abbey, *both parts, but first title in facsimile*
4to. 1622

322 Il Pastor Fido, or the Faithfull Shepheard, translated out of Italian into English
morocco, gilt edges, by Bedford (Evans' in 1825, £12) *very rare* *4to. Printed for Simon Waterson.* 1602
*** Prefixed are verses by S. Daniel, the poet.

323 W. (W.) Jewes Prophesy, or Newes from Rome of two mightie Armies, as well footemen as horsmen, the first of the great Sophy, the other of an Hebrew people, till this time not discovered, comming from the mountaines of Caspii, who pretend their warre is to recover the Land of Promise, and expell the Turks out of Christendome, translated out of Italian into English, 1607
black letter, large woodcut, part of imprint cut off, morocco by Bedford 1607
*** Only one other copy is known. See at the end a curious allusion to a Jew named Shylock.

324 Lupton (Thomas) Second Part and Knitting up of the Boke entituled, Too good to be true, wherein is continued the discourse of the wonderfull Lawes, commendable customes, and strange manners of the people of Mauqsun
black letter, a fine copy, but with a very small hole in one leaf of the Dedication, morocco, gilt edges, by Bedford
4to. Printed by Henry Binneman, 1581
*** This Second Part is quite a separate publication from Siquila, and is much the rarer of the two. A diligent search for it two years ago, for a literary purpose, failed to discover a copy in any public or private library in London. Its chief interest consists in its containing a story similar to the plot of Measure for Measure.

325 Greene's Ghost Haunting Conie-catchers, wherein is set downe the Arte of Humouring, the Arte of carrying Stones, and Blacke Robin's Kindnesse, with the Conceits of Doctor Pinch-backe, a notable Makeshift, ten times more pleasant then anything yet published of this matter
blackletter, First edition, *morocco gilt edges by Bedford*
4to. 1602

326 Greene (Robert) Defence of Conny-catching, or a Confutation of those two injurious pamphlets published by R. G. against the practitioners of many nimble-witted and mysticall Sciences, by Cuthbert Cunnycatcher, Licenciate in Whittington College
woodcut, black letter, *fine copy, morocco by Bedford*
4to. Printed by A. J. for Thomas Gubbins, 1592

GREENE (ROBERT) SECOND PART OF CONNY-CATCHING, con-
tayning the discovery of certaine wondrous Coosenages,
either superficiallie past over, or utterlie untouch in the
first, as the nature of the black Art, picking of Lockes,
coosenage at bowls, horsestealing, hooking at windows,
stealing of parcels, &c. with sundry pithy and pleasant
Tales

black letter, FIRST EDITION, *woodcuts, a beautiful copy,
morocco, gilt edges, by Bedford*
4to. *Printed by John Wolfe for William Wright,* 1591

₊ This first edition is believed to be unique, being undescribed by bibliographers, who derive their knowledge
of such an edition solely from an entry on the books of
the Stationers' Company. No copy of it is mentioned in
any catalogue we are acquainted with, and it contains
several more woodcuts than are found in the next impression, besides other variations. In contents, it may be
considered the most curious of all Greene's works.

328 Greene (Robert) Most Excellent History of Dorastus and
Fawnia, *in verse, no title*

₊ Only one other copy of this metrical version is known.
The story is the foundation of Shakespeare's Winter's
Tale.

329 Greene (R.) Quip for an Upstart Courtier, or a quaint dispute
betweene Velvet Breeches and Cloth Breeches, wherein is
plainly set downe the disorders in all Estates and Trades
woodcut, black letter, *morocco gilt edges by Bedford*
4to. 1620

330 GREENE (ROBERT) NOTABLE DISCOVERY OF COOSENAGE, now
daily practised by sundry lewd persons, called Connie-
catchers, and Crosse-byters, plainely laying open those
pernicious sleightes that hath brought many ignorant men
to confusion

black letter, *woodcuts, fine copy, morocco gilt edges by
Bedford* 4to. *Printed by John Wolfe,* 1591

331 GREENES NEWES BOTH FROM HEAVEN AND HELL, prohibited
the first for writing of Bookes, and banished out of the
last for displaying of Connycatchers. Commended to
the Presse by B. R. (Barnaby Rich)

black letter, *morocco by Bedford,*
4to. *Printed Anno Domini* 1593.

₊ The extreme rarity of this piece is well known. Mr.
Dyce never could meet with it ; it is in no public library,
nor in any sale catalogue we are acquainted with. It is
full of personal matter relating to Greene and notices
of his numerous works, distinctly proving that the curious
tracts on coneycatching were really written by him. The

5

purchaser's attention is drawn to two very slight def__
in sig. B, but the volume may on the whole be fair_
described as a fine perfect copy.

332 Shakespeare (W.) Late and Much Admired Play called _BARTON_
Pericles, Prince of Tyre, with the true Relation of the
whole History, adventures, and Fortunes of the sayd
Prince, written by William Shakespeare,
morocco gilt edges by Bedford,
4to. *Printed by I. N. for R. B., without place of sale,* 1630.
*** Only one other copy is known with this imprint. All
other copies that have been examined have the imprint in smaller type, as follows,—"London, Printed
by I. N. for R. B., and are to be sould at his shop in
Cheapside, at the signe of the Bible, 1630." See the
next lot.

333 Shakespeare (W.) Late and Much Admired Play called Pericles,
Prince of Tyre, &c., *large copy*
London, Printed by I. N. for R. B. and are to be sould at
his shop in Cheapside at the Signe of the Bible, 1630.

334 Shakespeare (W.) Wittie and Pleasant Comedie called the
Taming of the Shrew, as it was acted by his Majesties
Servants at the Blacke Friars and the Globe. Written by
Will. Shakespeare
FIRST EDITION.
4to. *Printed by W. S. for John Smethwicke,* 1631.
*** A remarkably fine copy of an edition almost invariably
found in bad condition. This edition has lately become
of great interest, from a discovery made by Mr. Collier,
in his last impression of Shakespeare, that the text is
prior to that in the first folio. It thus forms one of the
series of first editions.

335 Shakespeare (W.) Chronicle History of Henry the Fifth, with
his battell fought at Agincourt in France, together with
Ancient Pistoll. As it hath bene sundry times playd by
the Right Honourable the Lord Chamberlaine his Servants
fine copy, morocco, gilt edges, by Bedford. 4to.
Printed for T. P. 1608.

336 Shakespeare (William) First Part of the true and Honorable
History of the Life of Sir John Oldcastle, the good Lord
Cobham, as it hath bene lately acted by the Right Honor-
able the Earle of Notingham, Lord High Admirall of
England, his Servants. Written by William Shakespeare
FINE COPY, *morocco, gilt edges, by Bedford* 4to.
London, Printed for T. P. 1600

337 Shakespeare (William) Whole Contention betweene the two
Famous Houses, Lancaster and Yorke, with the Tragicall
ends of the good Duke Humfrey, Richard Duke of Yorke,

and King Henrie the Sixth. Divided into two parts, and newly corrected and enlarged. Written by William Shakespeare, Gent. *both parts complete*

morocco, gilt edges   *4to.*

Printed at London for T. P. n. d.

*** The date is supposed to be 1619. Loscombe's copy sold for £11 5s. The present is a fine copy, but a few of the head lines are slightly cut into.

338 Rich (Barnaby), Farewell to Militarie Profession, conteining very pleasant discourses fit for a peaceable time, gathered together for the onely delight of the courteous Gentle-women, both of England and Ireland, for whose onely pleasure they were collected together, and unto whom they are directed and dedicated

black letter, *morocco gilt edges by Bedford*

4to. Thomas Adams, 1606

17-0-0

*** A collection of early English novels, of great rarity, including one from which Shakespeare took his plot of Twelfth Night. Only two perfect copies are believed to be known, besides the present.

339 Shakespeare (William) Tragedie of King Richard the Second, with new additions of the Parliament Sceane, and the deposing of King Richard, as it hath been lately acted by the Kinges Majesties servants at the Globe, *fine, clean, firm copy*

morocco, gilt edges, by Bedford   *4to.*

Printed for Mathew Law, and are to be sold at his shop in Paules Churchyard, at the signe of the Foxe, 1615

32-10-0

*** The finest copy we have seen of this edition, which is generally found printed on thinner and inferior paper. After the first edition of 1597, this one ranks the next in literary interest, being that from which the copy in the first folio of 1623 was taken.

340 Shakespeare (William) Excellent History of the Merchant of Venice, with the extreme cruelty of Shylocke the Jew towards the saide Merchant in cutting a just pound of his flesh, and the obtaining of Portia by the choyse of three Caskets

morocco, gilt edges, by Bedford

4to. Printed by J. Roberts, 1600

21-0-0

*** This is now ascertained, from entries in the Stationers' Registers, to be the *first edition*. The present copy is an exceedingly desirable one, large, firm, and without a single defect.

2 —18— 341 Shakespeare (W.) Poems, *the frontispiece a reprint*
*a clean sound copy   Printed at London by Thos. Cotes,*1640

3—10— 342 Shakespeare (W.) Tragædy of Othello, the Moore of Venice,
as it hath beene divers times acted at the Globe and at
the Black-Friers, by his Majesties Servants
morocco, gilt edges, by Bedford
4*to.   Printed for William Leak,* 1655

4— - — 343 Shakespeare (W.) Most Excellent and Lamentable Tragedie of
Romeo and Juliet, as it hath been sundry times publikely
Acted by the King's Majesties Servants at the Globe
EDGES UNCUT, *morocco, by Bedford*
4*to.   Printed by R. Young,* 1637

1—1— 344 SHAKSPERIAN SCRAPS. A large Collection of Shaksperian
Pieces, Original Cuttings from Books, Slips, &c. Old
Music, some of the Editor's MS. of the new folio edition
of Shakespeare, Black-letter Fragments used in that
work, &c. &c. a very miscellaneous and curious collection

— 10 —6. 345 Shakespeare (W.) Merry Wives of Windsor, *imperfect,* 1619
—The Famous Victories of Henry the Fifth, *a fragment,*
1617—The First Part of the Contention of the two
Famous Houses of Yorke and Lancaster (part of the un-
dated edition of the Whole Contention)—The Second
Part of the Contention, *same edition, imperfect*—Hamlet,
no title, 1637

proposed. 346 Shakespeare. A large Collection of Fragments of the first
folio edition of Shakespeare   *folio. Lond.* 1623

do. 347 A large Elizabethan Oak Chest, of the Shaksperian period, the
front carved. "An empty trunk, o'erflourished by the
devil." —*Twelfth Night.*

—18— 348 Seal-ring, head of Shakespeare, temp. George II, an early, *Banto*
perhaps the earliest, specimen of the conventional head of
the Poet being used in this way.